Clouded Vision

Linwood Barclay

An Orion paperback

First published in Great Britain in 2011
by Orion Books Ltd
Orion House, 5 Upper St Martin's Lane,
London WC2H 9EA

An Hachette UK company

7 9 10 8 6

ADVICE: CONTAINS VIOLENT SCENES

A CIP catalogue record for this book is available from the British Library.

ISBN 978 1 4091 2125 1

Typeset at The Spartan Press Ltd,
Lymington, Hants

Printed in Great Britain by Clays Ltd,
St Ives plc

www.orionbooks.co.uk

For readers

Setting the Scene

Ellie

She'd been dreaming that she was already dead. Then, just before her dream came true, she opened her eyes.

With the little energy she had, she tried to move, but she was pinned down, tied in somehow. Tired, she lifted a bloody hand from her lap and her fingers felt the strap that ran across her chest. She knew its texture, its smoothness. A seat belt.

She was in a car, sitting in the front.

She looked around and it came to her that it was her own car. Yet she wasn't behind the steering wheel. She was strapped into the passenger seat.

She blinked a couple of times, thinking there must be something wrong with her eyes because she couldn't really make anything out. Then it became clear that it wasn't a problem with her sight.

It was night.

She gazed out through the windscreen, to see stars shining in the sky. It was a lovely evening, if she forgot about how all the blood was draining from her body.

It was hard for her to hold her head up, but with what strength she still had, she looked around. As she took in the starkness, the strangeness of where she was, she wondered if she might actually be dead already.

Maybe this was heaven? There was a certain peace about it. Everything was so white. There was a sliver of moon in the cloudless sky. It lit up the landscape, which was totally flat and seemed to go on forever.

Was her car parked on a snowy field? Far, far away, she thought she could make out something. There was a dark, uneven border running straight across the top of the whiteness. Trees, maybe? The thick, black line almost had the look of a – of a shoreline.

'What?' she said quietly to herself.

Slowly, she began to understand where she was. No – not *understand*. She was starting to *work out* where she was, but she couldn't *understand* it.

She was on ice.

The car was sitting on a frozen lake somewhere in the northern New England area of the US. And it was quite some way out, as far as she could tell.

'No, no, no, no, no,' she said to herself as she tried hard to think. It was only the middle of December. The temperatures had plunged a week ago. While it might have been cold enough for the lake to start freezing over, it certainly hadn't been cold long enough to make the ice thick enough to support a—

Crack.

She felt the front end of the car dip ever so slightly, probably no more than an inch. That would make sense. The car was heaviest at the front, where the engine was.

She knew she had to get out of this car. If the ice was able to support something as heavy as a car, at least for this long, surely it would keep her up if she could get herself out. She could start walking, whichever way would get her to the closest shore.

Could she even walk? She touched her hand to her belly. Everything she felt was warm, and wet. How many times had she been stabbed? That was what had happened, right? She could see the knife, the light catching the blade, and then—

The knife had gone into her twice, she thought. Then everything had faded to black.

Dead.

But she wasn't.

She must have had just a hint of a pulse. It must not have been noticed as she was put into the car and buckled in. Then she had been driven out here to the middle of this lake, where, someone must have figured, the car would soon go through the ice and sink to the bottom.

A car with a body inside it, dumped in a lake near the shore – someone might discover that too easily.

But a car with a body inside it that sank to the bottom out in the middle of a lake, what were the odds anyone would ever find that?

She knew she had to find the strength. She had to get out of this car now, before it went through the ice. Did she have her mobile? If she could call for help, they could come looking for her out on the ice. She wouldn't have to walk all the way back to—

Crack.

The car lurched forward. The way it was leaning, her view ahead now was snow-dusted ice instead of the far shore. The moon was casting enough light for her to see the inside of the car.

There was no sign of her handbag, which was where she kept her mobile. Whether she had a phone or not, it didn't change the fact that she had to get out of this car.

She had to get out right now.

She reached around to her side, looking for the button to release the seat belt. She found it and pressed with her thumb. The combined lap and shoulder strap began to move, catching briefly on her arm. She pulled it out of the way and the belt receded into the pillar between the back and front door.

Crack.

She reached down for the door handle and pulled. The door opened only slightly. It was enough for freezing-cold water to start rushing in around her feet.

'No, no,' she whispered.

As water started to fill the inside, the car tilted more. She had to put her hands flat on the dashboard to keep herself in the seat as the car shifted forward. With one hand on the dashboard, she pushed with the other on the door, but she couldn't get it to open. The front part of the door, at the bottom, was catching on the surface of the ice.

'Please, no.'

The last crack she heard was the loudest, echoing across the lake like a thunderclap.

The front end of the car dropped suddenly. Water rushed in, now swirling around her knees. Then it was at her waist. Next it reached her neck. Then everything became very black, and very cold, and then, in a strange way, very calm.

Her last thoughts were of her daughter, and the grandchild she would never see.

'Melissa,' she whispered.

And then the car was gone.

One

Keisha

Keisha Ceylon stared at the house and thought, sometimes you could tell, just by looking at a place, that there was hurt inside.

She was sitting in the car with the engine running so that she could keep the heater on. Keisha was sure her feelings about the house were not affected by what she already knew. She told herself that if she'd just been walking past, and had merely glanced at this home, she'd have picked up something.

Despair. Concern. Fear.

All the same, there wasn't anything to mark this house out from any other on the street. The only difference was that the inch of snow that had fallen overnight had not been cleared from the drive, nor from the path up to the front door. In addition, the curtains were drawn and the blinds shut.

Keisha thought about what the man who lived in the house must be feeling. How was he dealing with it? Was he at the point where he would be desperate enough to accept, and pay, for the very special service she could provide?

She believed her timing was about right. This was always the tricky part – knowing when to make a move. You couldn't act too quickly, but you didn't want to leave it too late, either. If you waited too long, the police might actually find a body. If that happened, no upset relative was going to care what kind of visions Keisha Ceylon might be having that would lead them to the body. A fat lot of good her visions would do then.

You had to get hold of these people while they still had hope. As long as they had hope, they were willing to try anything and throw their *money* at anything. This was even more true when all the usual methods – door-to-door questions, sniffer dogs, patrols from the air, searches of the local area – hadn't found anything.

That's when the relatives were open to something a bit out of the ordinary. They might warm to a nice lady who showed up on their doorstep and said, 'I have a gift, and I want to share it with you.'

For a price, of course.

The other important thing about timing was the competition. If Keisha didn't move fast enough, if she didn't get to the family soon, she ran the risk of getting beaten by Winona Simpson.

That bitch.

Winona Simpson had been doing this for nearly as long as Keisha – the whole 'I have a vision' thing. The difference was that Winona really *believed*. The woman was actually convinced she'd been blessed with some special power – an ability to see things that no one else could see. It drove Keisha nuts. What's more, because Winona really believed it was her mission to help people in their time of need, she always charged less than Keisha for her work.

'I'm not in this to make money,' she'd once told Keisha. It was when they'd both had their sights set on a couple whose two-year-old daughter had wandered away and was believed to have drowned in a creek a year and a half ago. 'I want to help these people. All I ask is that they cover my expenses, which are minimal.'

'You must be joking,' Keisha'd told her.

Keisha had lost out that time, because Winona had already spoken to the parents.

She told them where she believed the child was. However, before they could get to the location, a father and son playing with a radio-controlled boat found the child's body lodged under a bridge. It was exactly where Winona had said it would be.

Keisha wondered how the hell she did it. She didn't want to believe that Winona really had the gift, but some things were very hard to explain. Keisha was pretty sure Winona had not beaten her this time around.

The missing woman's name was Eleanor Garfield. She was, according to the news reports, white, forty-one years old and five foot three. She weighed about a hundred and fifty pounds and had short black hair and brown eyes.

Everyone called her Ellie.

She was last seen, according to her husband Wendell, on Thursday evening, at about seven o'clock. She got in her car, a silver Nissan, with the intention of going to the grocery store to pick up the things they needed for the week. Ellie Garfield had a job in the offices of the local board of education, and she didn't like to leave all her chores to the weekend. She wanted Saturday and Sunday to be without such jobs. To her way of thinking, the weekend actually began on Friday night.

So Thursday night was for running errands.

That way, come Friday, she could have a long soak in a hot bath. After that, she'd slip into her pyjamas and pink bathrobe and park herself in front of the television. It was mostly for background noise, because she rarely had her eyes on it. Her main focus was her knitting.

Knitting had always been a hobby for her, although she hadn't shown much interest in it over the last few years. According to a newspaper reporter who had tried to capture the essence of this missing woman, Ellie had gone back to it when she learned she was going to become a grandmother. She had been making baby booties and socks and a couple of sweaters. 'I'm knitting away as if my life depended on it,' she'd told one of her friends.

But this particular week, Ellie Garfield did not make it to Friday night.

Nor did she, by all accounts, make it to the store on Thursday. None of the grocery store staff, who knew Ellie Garfield by sight, if not by name, recalled seeing her. There was no record that her credit card, which she preferred to using cash, had been used that evening. Her card had not been used since. Her car was not picked up on the closed-circuit cameras that kept watch over the grocery store car park.

Keisha had read the news stories on the woman's disappearance and had seen reports on television. It looked to her as if the police didn't know what to make of it. Had Ellie met with foul play? Did she begin by intending to go to the grocery store and decide instead to just keep on driving? Had she wanted to leave her old life behind and start a new one?

That seemed unlikely, especially as she was about to have her first grandchild. What woman disappears on the eve of something like that?

Police floated the theory that she was the victim of a car-jacking. There had been three incidents in the last year where a female driver, who had come to a stop at a traffic light, had been pulled from the car. The car-jacker – believed to be the same man in all three cases – had then driven off in the car. The women had been shaken up, but not seriously hurt.

Maybe Ellie Garfield had run into the same man but, this time, things had become violent.

On Saturday, Wendell Garfield went before the television cameras, his pregnant daughter at his side. The girl was crying too much to say anything, but Wendell held back his tears long enough to make his plea.

'I just want to say, honey, if you're watching,

please, please come home. We love you and we miss you and we just want you back. And . . . and, if something has happened to . . . if someone has done something to you, then I make this appeal to whoever has done this . . . I'm asking you, please let us know what's happened to Ellie. Please let us know where she is, that she's OK . . . Just tell us something . . . I . . . I . . .'

At that point he turned away from the camera, overcome.

Keisha almost shed a tear herself. It was time to make her move. She was willing to bet her Tarot cards and Ouija board that Winona was watching this, thinking the same thing.

So that evening, Keisha took a drive past the Garfield home, which was set back from the street in a heavily wooded neighbourhood. She got the lay of the land, as it were. She wanted to see whether the place was surrounded with police cars, marked or unmarked. Was Winona's car, a Toyota Prius, on the street? Keisha saw what she believed was one unmarked police car, but that was it.

She decided to make her move on Sunday morning, first thing.

If you did this enough, it got pretty easy. It was the people themselves who fed you the vision. You started off vaguely, with something like, 'I see a house . . . a white house with a fence out front . . .'

And then they'd say, 'A white house? Wait, wait, didn't Aunt Gwen live in a white house?'

Someone else would say, 'That's right, she did!'

Then, picking up the past tense, you said, 'And this Aunt Gwen, I'm sensing . . . I'm sensing she's passed on.'

And they said, 'Oh my God, that's right, she has!'

The key was to listen and have them give you the clues. If you gave them something to latch on to, then you would be fine.

It wouldn't be any different with Wendell Garfield.

However, not everyone was convinced. There had been one woman, a few years ago. Her parents and brother had disappeared one night twenty-five years earlier when she was only fourteen. Cynthia, that was her name. You'd have thought that if there was *anyone* who'd be willing to take a leap of faith with someone like Keisha, it would have been this woman. They even got as far as the TV studio, where they were going to film Keisha outlining her vision for Cynthia. The moment she raised the issue of being paid, everything came to a standstill. It was the husband, the teacher, who protested. As soon as Keisha wanted to be paid for her services, he started saying that she was some kind of con artist or something.

The prick.

Wendell Garfield was different. She had a good feeling about him from the TV appearance.

Keisha was up early on Sunday. She'd spent time the night before choosing the right outfit. It must be nothing too flashy, but you needed something quirky somewhere. People thought that, if you could talk to the dead, see into unseen dimensions, you had to be a little off your rocker, right? It was *expected*. So she wore earrings that looked like tiny green parrots.

She got into her Toyota and used the windscreen wipers to clear the dusting of snow from the previous night. When she got to the Garfield house, she was relieved to see no police cars out front. It was always better if you could do this without the cops. They'd probably offer the opinion that you might as well set your cash on fire as hand it over to some pretend psychic.

Keisha sat in the car a moment, getting her head in the right space.

She was ready.

It was time to go in and explain to the frantic husband that she could help him in his hour of need. She could be his *instrument* to help determine what had happened to his wife Ellie.

Keisha had *seen* something. She'd had a *vision.* It very possibly held the answer to why his wife of twenty-one years had been missing for three nights now.

It was a vision that she would be happy to share with him.

For the right price.

Keisha Ceylon took a deep breath, took one last look at her lipstick in the rear-view mirror, and opened the car door.

It was time for the show to begin.

Two
Wendell

'So, what are you telling me, that there's been nothing, nothing at all?' Wendell Garfield said into the phone. 'I thought, I really thought someone . . . Well, if you hear anything, anything at *all*, please, please call me. I'm desperate for any kind of news.'

He replaced the receiver in its cradle. He had decided, when he got up that morning, that he would call the police first thing. He would ask whether the news conference that he and his daughter had done yesterday had produced any useful tip offs.

The officer he'd just spoken to was not the one in charge of the investigation, but he claimed to know what was happening. There had been only about half a dozen calls to the special hotline that the police had set up. None of them had been considered useful.

Garfield decided to make himself some tea, thinking it would help calm him. He hadn't slept more than a few minutes overnight. He was trying to work out just how much sleep he'd had since Thursday, when this had all started. It was no more than five, six hours maybe. Melissa had probably had a little more than that, if only because the pregnancy made her so tired.

Garfield hadn't wanted his daughter to be part of the press conference. He'd told the police he wasn't sure she could handle the stress. She was seven months' pregnant, and her mother was missing. Now they wanted her to be on the six o'clock news?

'I don't want to put her through that,' he'd told the police.

Yet it was Melissa herself who insisted she appear alongside her father. 'We'll do it together, Dad,' she told him. 'Everyone needs to know we want Mom to be found and that we want her to come home.'

With some reluctance, he agreed, but only if he did all the talking. As it turned out, once the lights were on and the cameras were in their faces, Melissa went to pieces. She managed only to splutter, 'Mommy, please come back to us,' before she dissolved into tears and put her face into her father's chest. Even he wasn't able to say very much, just that they loved Ellie very much and wanted her to come home.

Then he made his appeal to anyone out there who might know anything to do with his wife's disappearance. Please, tell us what's happened. Send Ellie home to us.

And then he lost it, too.

He could hear murmurs among some of the news people, phrases like 'good stuff' and 'perfect' and 'awesome'.

What disgusting human beings, Garfield thought.

He took Melissa home with him and tried to get her to eat something. 'It's going to be OK,' he told her. 'Everything's going to be OK. We'll get through this.'

She sat there at the kitchen table, her head nearly on the table. 'Oh, Daddy . . .'

'Trust me,' he said.

She stayed overnight, but around six o'clock in the morning said she wanted to go back to her apartment across town. Garfield wasn't so sure that was a good idea, but Melissa said she could handle it. She wasn't going to stay there. She'd still come back later on and stay overnight in the room she used to live in. All the same, she needed some time by herself, to think. Melissa shared the apartment with her friend Olivia, but Olivia was away right now, visiting her parents in Denver.

Garfield was awake at six – he'd never been asleep – and said he would drive his daughter back to her place.

He parked in front of the apartment, which was actually the top floor of an old house with a separate entrance.

Garfield said, 'Are you sure you're going to be OK? Do you want me to wait?'

Melissa said, no.

Even though she was only nineteen, Melissa had been living away from home for three years. She was the first to admit she'd been a difficult teenager from the beginning. She drank, used drugs and slept around. She ignored the limits her parents attempted to set for her.

When she was sixteen, Ellie and Wendell decided they could take no more. They gave her a stark choice. She must live by the rules of their house, or get out.

She chose to get out.

Melissa found a place to live with Olivia. She dropped out of school and got a job as a waitress at Denny's. It turned out that getting kicked out of her parents' house was the best thing that had ever happened to her. It forced her to get her act together. She didn't have anyone else to take care of her, so she had to take care of herself.

She started to become responsible. Whoever would have guessed?

Ellie and Wendell were quietly optimistic. Once Melissa got her head screwed on, they thought, she could go back and finish school. If she did well enough, she might even have a chance of going to college, Ellie mused one evening. Maybe she'd even think about becoming a vet. She reminded Wendell of how, when their daughter was little, she had said one day she'd love to work with animals and—

'For God's sake, Ellie, let's not get ahead of ourselves,' Wendell said.

Melissa used to come over for dinner. Some of these get-togethers went better than others. One night, Melissa would tell them about how she was getting her life back on track. Her parents would nod and try to be encouraging. Yet on another night, Ellie, keen to see her daughter get her life back on track, would start pushing.

She'd tell her daughter it was time – *now* – to stop being 'nothing more than a waitress'. Melissa should go back to school and make something of herself. Did Melissa have any idea just how embarrassing it was for her mother, an employee of the board of education, to have a daughter who was a dropout? Melissa hadn't even finished her final year at school. How long was she expected to wait before seeing her daughter get on a path where she would amount to something?

Then they'd start fighting and Melissa would storm out. Before she did so, she would ask out loud how she'd managed to live in this house for so long without blowing her brains out.

It always took a few days for the dust to settle.

Ellie and Wendell still kept their fingers crossed that Melissa was growing up. She held on to her waitressing job. She was saving some money, even if not a lot. It was only about twenty-five dollars a week, but it was something. Then one day, when talking to her mother on the phone, Melissa happened to mention that she'd looked at a college website to see what grades you needed to enrol in the course to become a vet.

Ellie was beside herself with joy when she told Wendell the news.

'Isn't it wonderful?' she asked. 'She's growing

up, that's what she's doing. She's growing up and thinking about the future.'

What neither Ellie or Wendell had counted on was that the immediate future would include a baby.

Melissa was already three months' pregnant when she broke the news to her parents. They did not, to say the least, take it well, but Wendell tried to find the silver lining. Maybe this meant Melissa would get married. She'd be a very young mother, but at least it would mean she had a man in her life, a man who could look after her. Wouldn't that take some of the pressure off Ellie and him?

Then they found out about the man. It soon became clear that the only thing that might be worse than Melissa having this baby with no father on the scene would be having this baby *with* the father on the scene.

His name was Lester Cody. He was thirty years old and a regular customer at Denny's. He'd never hung on to a job longer than three months, and none of them had ever paid a penny more than the minimum wage. He always ended up injured. He hurt his back, damaged his shoulder or sprained his ankle. Yet luckily, no matter how badly he might have gotten hurt, he could still play his Nintendo Wii. He lived in his parents' basement and still had Spider-Man posters on his bedroom wall. His favourite hat was adorned with a plastic dog turd.

Ellie cried for the better part of a week before she was able to accept the situation. Her daughter was really going to have this child, she was not going to marry Lester Cody, and Ellie was going to become a grandmother.

This baby's coming, she realised. There's not a damn thing I can do about it. So, she took up her knitting again.

Sometimes, it was all more than Wendell Garfield could stand. There was tension between his wife and daughter, and Ellie wanted to have constant debates with him about what their girl was going to do with her life. Now, there was all this new talk about the baby. How would Melissa manage? Would she need to move back home? Would the man who got her pregnant step up to the plate and accept some responsibility?

The discussions never stopped.

Wendell Garfield wondered if all this had driven him into the arms of Laci Harmon. Perhaps it would have happened anyway.

Three
Wendell

Wendell and Laci both worked at the Home Depot hardware store, him primarily in plumbing, and her over in home lighting fixtures. They'd had coffee breaks together, talking about their families, the joys and – mostly – heartaches of raising kids. She had two boys aged fifteen and seventeen who did nothing but fight with one another. Laci confessed once, only half jokingly, that she wished they'd have one final free-for-all battle and kill each other.

Wendell laughed. He said he knew exactly how she felt.

He always found reasons to stroll through the lighting section.

Laci often seemed to be passing through the plumbing supplies aisle.

It started with friendly teasing, then comments with double meanings. When Laci wandered by, she'd narrow her eyes and say she needed help with her plumbing. When Garfield was over in light fixtures, he'd bump into Laci on purpose and say he wondered if she could help him keep his light switch in the up position.

It was all in fun.

One day Wendell had been asked to assemble, for display purposes, a vinyl-sided garden shed. He was inside the nearly finished structure, tightening up some bolts to make sure the thing wouldn't blow down in the wind. Suddenly Laci Harmon stepped inside, slid the door shut behind her, and placed his right hand on her left breast.

It was a Thursday. That night, when Ellie was doing the weekly grocery shopping, Garfield slipped away from home and met Laci at a Day's Inn hotel. They had been finding ways to get together once or twice a week since then, always in places that were nicer than a vinyl-sided garden shed, although not always by much. One of these places was Laci's Dodge minivan, for example. Garfield longed for these moments away from home, away from the endless stresses that Ellie and Melissa provided.

*

He'd only just put down the phone from speaking with the police when it rang again.

'Hello?'

'Oh, Wen, I just had to get in touch.'

'Laci, this isn't a good time.'

'But I can't stop thinking about you, about what you must be going through,' she said. She wasn't whispering, which told Garfield that she was alone in her house.

'Where are your husband and the boys?' he asked her.

'They're out. It's just me here,' Laci said. 'Wendell, you have to talk to me.'

'What do you want me to say?'

'Have they found out anything? Do the police know what happened? I saw the press conference. I watched it at six o'clock, and I watched it again at eleven. It was very moving. You were very good, if you know what I mean. You held it together really well. I think, if anyone knew anything, if they knew anything at all, they'd call the hotline if they saw your appeal.'

'I was just speaking to the police,' Garfield said. 'They haven't received any good tips.'

'I feel . . . I feel so . . . It's hard to explain,' Laci said. 'I feel guilty in a way, you know?

Because of what we've been doing, behind her back.'

'Those things don't have anything to do with each other.'

'I know that, but I keep thinking, what if someone finds out? What if someone finds out what's going on between us? They might think it has something to do with what's happened to Ellie. And if, God forbid, something has actually happened to Ellie, then how is it going to look if—'

'Laci, please, don't go there,' he said. 'Maybe she just decided to go away for a while, to clear her head.'

'Is that what you think?'

'I don't know what to think, but I suppose it's a possibility. I mean, they haven't found her car or anything. If something had happened to her around here, you'd think they'd have at least found her car. We're into the third day now.'

'So you think she just decided to drive away? To Florida or something?'

'Laci, I don't know, *OK*? I have no idea whatsoever.'

His tone stopped Laci for a second. 'You don't have to get angry with me.'

'I'm going through a lot right now. I'm just trying to keep it together.'

'How's Melissa coping?'

'Not so well.'

'What about the man who got her pregnant? Is he still in the picture? Can he be there for Melissa at a time like this?'

'She hasn't heard from him. Honestly, I don't think it would make things any easier for us if he was around.'

'I was just— Oh my God, I just thought of something,' she said.

'What?'

'The police aren't tapping your phone, are they? They're not listening in?'

He felt a chill run down his spine. Could they be? He could kick himself. It hadn't even occurred to him until she mentioned it. He'd been doing such a good job, being the distraught husband. He hadn't thought there was any reason for the police to be bugging his phone. Sure, he knew the cops would probably be looking at him sooner or later, but he didn't believe he'd given any sign that he was in any way responsible for his wife's disappearance.

'I mean, if they hear us, and know we've been seeing each other, then—'

'Hang up, Laci,' he said.

'—then they might think that you had something to do with it, you know, so that you could spend your life with me and—'

He slammed down the phone. If the police had been listening, the damage had been done. They'd know he'd been having an affair. They'd know he and Laci had been seeing each other for weeks now.

It was not good, not good at all.

Wendell was totally rattled. He tried to calm himself and tell himself he was going to get through this. He just needed to keep his wits about him. Even if the police found out he'd been sleeping with Laci, it didn't have to mean he'd had anything to do with this business about his wife.

They hadn't found a body or her car.

And he was as sure as he could be that they never would.

'Pull yourself together,' he told himself.

The doorbell rang.

Hell, he thought. The cops really *were* listening to his phone. Now they wanted to question him about Laci, about whether he killed his wife to be with another woman.

He took a couple of deep breaths, composed himself, and strode through the living room to the front door. He pulled the curtain back first, to see who it was.

It was not the police. It was a woman, with green parrot earrings.

Four
Keisha

Keisha Ceylon was ready with her 'I feel your pain' smile. First impressions were everything. You had to come across, first and foremost, as sincere. So you couldn't overdo the smile. It had to be held back. You didn't want to show any teeth. No empty-headed, sweet and sickly smile that looked as if it had been pasted on. You had to get into the moment. You had to *believe* you were on a mission. Most of all, you had to look as though you were sorry to even be here, and that this really was the last place on earth you wanted to be.

Yet you were *compelled* to be here. You simply had no choice.

She saw the man pull back the curtain to get a look at her and gave him the smile. It was almost regretful.

Then the door opened.

'Yes?' he said.

'Mr Garfield?'

'That's right.' He leaned out of the door, looking past her down to the street.

'My name is Keisha Ceylon. I'm so sorry to trouble you at a time like this.' She extended a hand. The man hesitated before he took it.

'Yes, well, this is a very stressful time. Who are you . . . who are you with?'

Keisha guessed, with those parrots dangling from her earlobes, that Wendell wasn't going to take her for some plainclothes detective.

'I guess I'm what you'd call a consultant,' she said.

'For who?'

'I work for people who find themselves in situations such as yours, Mr Garfield.'

'You're, what, a private detective?'

'No. Perhaps, if I could come inside, I could explain it better to you?'

When you were still on the front step, they could slam the door in your face. However, once you were in the house, it was harder for them to get rid of you. She could see he was thinking about it.

After a moment's hesitation, he opened the door wide. 'Of course, come in.'

He led her into the living room and invited her to take one of the chairs across from the settee, which was where he sat.

'What was your name again?' he asked.

'Keisha Ceylon. Perhaps you've heard of me.'

Before she could sit down, she had to move a ball of green wool that was speared through with two blue, foot-long knitting needles. She tucked the bundle over to the edge of the chair.

'I . . . I can't say that I have. What is it that you do? I mean, what's the nature of your consulting?'

'As I said, I offer my services to people when they're dealing with the kind of crisis that you're currently going through.'

'Missing wives?'

'Well, any kind of missing person. Do you mind if I ask you a couple of questions first?'

'I suppose not.'

'I know you and your daughter made yourself available to the media yesterday to outline your concerns about Mrs Garfield.'

'That's right.'

'What sort of tips have the police received since then?'

Wendell shook his head. 'Nothing.'

Keisha nodded in sympathy, as though this was about what she expected. 'And what other efforts have the police been making in trying to find Mrs Garfield?'

'Well, they've been trying to trace her

movements since she left here Thursday night. That's the night she does the grocery shopping, but she never went to the store.'

'Yes, I knew that.'

'And her credit cards haven't been used. I know they've been showing her picture in all the places she usually goes, as well as talking to her friends and people she works with. All the things you might expect.'

Another sympathetic nod. 'But so far, there are no leads. Is that what you're telling me, Mr Garfield?'

'It would seem so,' he said.

Keisha Ceylon paused for what she thought was a suitably dramatic period of time, and then said, 'I believe I can help you where the police cannot.'

'How's that?'

'The police have employed all the typical methods that you would expect,' she said. 'They do what they do, but they are not trained to – what's the phrase? To think outside the box. What I offer is something more out of the ordinary.'

'And what is that, exactly?'

She looked him in the eye. 'I see things, Mr Garfield.'

His mouth opened, but he was briefly at a loss for words. Finally, he said, 'I'm sorry?'

'I can see things,' she repeated. 'Let me make this as simple and as clear as I can. Mr Garfield, I have visions.'

A small laugh erupted from him. 'Visions?'

Keisha was very careful to maintain her cool. Don't get defensive. Don't overplay your hand. 'Yes,' she said simply. She would play for time and make him ask the questions.

'What, uh, what kind of visions?'

'I've had this gift – if you can call it that, I'm not really sure – since I was a child, Mr Garfield. I have visions of people in distress.'

'Distress,' he said quietly. 'Really.'

'Yes,' she said again.

'And you've had a *vision* of my wife? In distress?'

She nodded solemnly. 'Yes, I have.'

'I see.' A bemused smile crossed his lips. Keisha had expected this. 'And you've decided to share this vision with *me*, and not the police.'

'As I'm sure you can understand, Mr Garfield, the police are often not receptive to people with my talents. It's not just that they're sceptical. When I'm able to make progress where they have not, they feel it reflects badly on them. So I directly approach the family involved.'

'Of course you do,' he said. 'And how is it you get these visions? Do you have, like, a TV aerial built into your head or something?'

She smiled. 'I wish I could answer your question in a way that someone could understand. If I knew how these visions come to me, I might be able to find a way to turn them off.'

'So it's a curse as well as a blessing,' he said.

Keisha ignored the sarcasm. 'Yes, a bit like that. Let me tell you a story. One night, about three years ago, I was driving to the shopping mall. I was just minding my own business when this . . . image came into my head. All of a sudden I could barely see the road in front of me. It was as though the view before me had turned into a movie screen.

'I saw this girl, who couldn't have been more than five or six. She was in a bedroom, but it was not a little girl's bedroom. There were no dolls or playhouses or anything like that. The room was decorated with sports memorabilia. There were trophies, posters of football players on the wall, a catcher's mitt on the desk, and a baseball bat leaning against the wall in the corner. This little girl was crying, saying she wanted to go home, pleading to someone to let her leave. Then there was a man's voice, and he was saying, not yet, you can't go home yet, not until we get to know each other a little better.'

She took a breath. Garfield was trying to look neutral, but Keisha could tell she had him hooked.

'Well, I nearly drove off the road. I slammed on the brakes and pulled over to the hard shoulder. By then, this vision, these images, had vanished, like smoke that had been blown away. However, I knew what I'd seen. I'd seen a little girl in trouble, a little girl who was being held against her will.

'So, in this particular situation, because I did not know who the actual people involved were, I made a decision to go to the police. I called them and said, "Are you working on a missing girl case? Is there perhaps something you haven't yet made a statement about?" Well, they were quite taken aback. They said they really couldn't give out that kind of information. And I said, "Is the girl about six years old? And was she last seen wearing a shirt with a *Sesame Street* character on it?" Well, now I had their attention.

'They sent out a detective to talk to me, and he didn't believe in visions any more than I would imagine you do. I think maybe they were thinking I might have actually had something to do with this girl's disappearance, because how else could I know those kinds of details? But I said to him, talk to the family, find out who they know who's really into sports, who's won lots of trophies, particularly football trophies, maybe even baseball.

'The detective said, yeah, sure, we'll get right on that, as if he was humouring me. Then he left and made some calls. Within the hour, the police had gone to the home of a neighbour who fitted that description, and they rescued that little girl. They got to her just in time.' Keisha paused. 'Her name was Nina. And last week she celebrated her ninth birthday. She was alive, and well.'

Total bullshit.

Keisha clasped her hands together and rested them in her lap, never taking her eyes off Wendell.

'Would you like to call Nina's father?' she asked. 'I think I could arrange that.'

Keisha didn't think he'd take her up on the offer, but if he did, she had Larson, her boyfriend, on standby to take the call.

'No, no, that's OK,' Garfield said. 'That's quite a tale.'

Keisha looked away and down at her hands, trying to be modest.

'But I totally understand,' she said, 'if you'd like me to leave. Perhaps you think I am a con artist. There are plenty out there, believe me. I don't know whether you've been contacted by a Winona Simpson, but she's definitely one to watch out for. If you don't want me to share my vision with you, I'll leave right now and you won't hear from me again. I just want to say, I hope the police find your wife soon, Mr Garfield, so that you and your daughter can get your lives back to normal.'

She stood up. Garfield was on his feet, too, and when Keisha extended her hand once again he took it right away.

'Thank you for your time, and I'm so sorry to have troubled you.'

'What will you do?' he said. 'I mean, if you've had this so-called vision, and I'm not the kind of person who believes in that sort of thing, what will you do now?'

'I suppose,' she said, 'I'll go and tell the police what I know, and see if there's anyone there who cares. Sometimes, though, that has a way of backfiring. It doesn't always work out the way it did with Nina. I've found that the police have a tendency to be hostile, and the tips you give them will end up being the last one they follow. I hope, for your wife's sake, that they don't take that attitude.'

'So you're going to the police,' he said, more to himself than to Keisha.

'Again, thank you for—'

'Sit down. You might as well tell me how this works.'

Five
Wendell

Wendell Garfield didn't know what the hell to make of this woman. Did Keisha Ceylon really have visions? The story about that little girl was pretty convincing, but it wasn't enough to persuade him Keisha was genuine. There was something about her, though, that was hard to dismiss.

His mind raced through the possibilities. The woman was trying to get money out of him, plain and simple. He had a feeling that, even though they hadn't gotten around to the topic of money, it was coming. What better target than a husband desperate to find out what had happened to his missing wife?

Perhaps plenty of people in his position would be willing to engage a psychic, a medium – whatever this woman wanted to call herself. This might be so even if they believed, at best, that there was only a one in a million chance that she really knew anything. Isn't that what someone who truly loved his wife would do?

Or maybe she wasn't trying to con him. Maybe she really did have visions. Maybe she truly believed she had some kind of connection to people in trouble, and was here out of a sincere wish to help him. However, maybe what she had wasn't a gift. Maybe she was a madwoman, with delusions. Her visions might be nothing more than the product of a twisted mind. In short, perhaps she was just hallucinating.

And then, of course, there was a third possibility: that she was the real thing.

Garfield considered that prospect highly unlikely. But what if, somehow, for reasons he did not yet understand, she was on to something? Did he want her talking to the police?

Not really.

The smartest course, for now, seemed to be to hear her out. He would hear what she had to say.

Once Keisha was back in the chair, with Wendell sitting across from her, he said, 'First of all, let me apologise if I was at all rude earlier.'

'Not at all. I understand that what I do, the

talent I have, is difficult for many people to get their heads around.'

'Yes, well, I have to admit, I have my doubts. But then again, I very much want to know what's happened to Ellie. I need to find out where she is. I want her to come home. I suppose it doesn't make sense to discount what you have to say until I've had a chance to hear it.'

Keisha smiled and nodded. 'I think that's very wise of you.'

'So, if you want to tell me your vision, then, what the hell, let's hear it.'

'I truly value you being open-minded about this. I would have felt terrible, not being able to help you in your time of need.'

'OK, then. Go ahead.'

'There is one other matter to deal with first.'

Here we go, he thought.

'This gift that I have is also my livelihood,' Keisha explained. 'I'm sure, if you were to hire a private detective to assist you in finding your wife, you wouldn't expect him to put in his time without being paid for it?'

'Of course not.'

'I'm pleased to hear you say that.'

'And what sort of money are we talking here, Ms Ceylon?' he asked.

'One thousand dollars,' she said, not being the least bit shy about it.

His eyebrows went up. 'You're not serious.'

'I have a rare gift,' Keisha said. 'I believe it's worth much more, but it would be my pleasure to help you for that sum, which I think is quite reasonable.'

He thought about it. 'I'm not a rich man.'

'I understand,' she said. 'I took that into account when I quoted that fee.'

'I see. There's a sliding scale? You take a look at the house and the kind of cars in the driveway, and if you see a BMW you jack the price up? You decide what the market will bear and so forth?'

Keisha started to get up. 'I think I'll just be on my way, Mr Garfield, if that's OK with—'

'How about this?' he said. 'You give me a hint of what your vision was all about, and if it sounds credible to me, then I'll give you five hundred dollars. If the information you have leads to my finding Ellie, I'll pay you another five hundred dollars.'

She considered his words for a moment, and then said, 'I will tell you a bit about my vision, and if you wish to hear more, I will tell you everything for the full amount. One thousand dollars.'

He let out a long sigh. He could only imagine what she must be thinking. His wife is missing, and he's going back and forth with her as if he's buying a new Ford. He was worried how that might look, so he said, 'All right then, we have a deal.'

'I'm very pleased,' she said. 'Not just because we've reached a satisfactory arrangement, but because I do very much want to be able to help you.'

'Yeah, yeah, fine.'

'Do you have something of your wife's that I might be able to hold?'

'What for?'

'It helps.'

'I thought you'd already had your vision. I don't understand why you need something of my wife's to hold on to.'

'It's all part of the process. Some of the fuzzier details in my vision may come into sharper focus if I can hold something that belongs to the person, something that's come into close contact with them.'

'What do you need?'

'An article of clothing would be best.'

'Like her bathrobe or something?'

Keisha nodded. Garfield excused himself and went upstairs. A moment later he was coming back down the stairs with a pink robe in his hands. It was faded and tattered from many years of wear.

'Thank you,' Keisha said, placing the robe in her lap and laying both hands on it. She ran her fingertips over the material and closed her eyes.

Several seconds went by without her saying a word. Finally, Garfield interrupted her trance state and said, 'Are you getting anything or what?'

'Just a moment.' She opened her eyes. 'I'm feeling some . . . tingling.'

'Tingling?'

'It's a little bit like when the hairs go up on the back of your neck. That's when I know I'm starting to sense something.'

'What? What are you sensing?'

'Your wife, she's . . .'

'She's what?'

'She's cold,' Keisha said. 'Your wife is very, very cold.'

Six

Keisha

While Keisha was seeing if Wendell would take the bait, giving her a chance to reel him in, she was thinking about her starting point. Her plan was to cast a wide net to begin with, then narrow the focus. Why not start with the weather?

It was winter, after all. *Everybody* was cold. Wherever Ellie Garfield was, it only stood to reason she'd be feeling chilled. OK, maybe that wasn't true. The night Wendell's wife disappeared she could have steered her car south and headed straight to Florida. She could have been there in a day, and by now might be working on a pretty decent tan.

However, Keisha wasn't all that concerned with where this man's wife really was. She just wanted to offer him some possibilities and, in return, make her money.

'What do you mean, cold?' Garfield asked, seeming, for the first time, intrigued.

'Just what I said. She's very cold. Did she take a jacket with her when she left Thursday night?'

'A jacket? Of course she'd have taken a jacket. She wouldn't have left the house without a jacket. Not at this time of year.'

Keisha nodded. 'I'm still picking up that she's cold. Not just, you know, a little bit cold. I mean, chilled to the bone. Maybe it wasn't a warm enough coat. Or maybe . . . maybe she lost her coat?'

'I don't see how she would lose her coat. Once you go outside, you know you need it.' He sank back into the settee, looking annoyed. 'I don't see that this is very helpful.'

'I can come back to it,' she said. 'Maybe, as I start picking up other things, the part about her being cold will take on more meaning.'

'I thought you had a vision. Why don't you just tell me what the vision was instead of rubbing your hands all over my wife's robe?'

'Please, Mr Garfield, it's not as though my vision was an episode of *Seinfeld* and I can just tell you what I watched. There are flashes, images, like fleeting snapshots. It's a little like dumping a shoebox full of snapshots on to a table. They're in a jumble, in no particular order. What I'm trying to do is like sorting those photos. Sitting here, now, in your wife's home, holding something that touched her, I can start piecing together those images, like a jigsaw puzzle.'

'You're pulling a fast one here. I think—'

'Melissa.'

'What?'

'Melissa. That's your daughter's name, correct?'

'That's no big trick. Her name's been in the paper.'

'I'm not trying to impress you with knowing her name, Mr Garfield. I'm trying to tell you about the images, the flashes.'

Garfield looked as though he'd been told off. 'I'm sorry. Go ahead.'

'Melissa is terribly troubled.'

'Well, of course.'

'But this goes beyond what you would expect a daughter to feel when her mother goes missing.'

Garfield leaned forward and placed his elbows on his knees. He seemed really interested now. Keisha thought maybe she'd struck some sort of nerve here. All she was doing, really, so far, was telling Garfield things he already knew, things everyone knew. It was winter. He had a pregnant daughter. It was logical she'd be upset. In another minute or so she'd get to the next stunningly obvious thing – the car. But first, she wanted to sound Garfield out about his daughter's pregnancy, which was pretty hard to miss during the TV coverage.

'What do you mean, it goes beyond?' he asked.

'Something about the baby . . .'

'What about the baby?'

'Tell me about the father,' Keisha said. She was turning it around, letting him do some of the work, and feeding her a few more nuggets to work with at the same time.

'Lester Cody. A useless son of a bitch.' Wendell Garfield shook his head in anger and frustration. 'He's thirty years old, has no job, and lives at home with his parents. When we learned Melissa was pregnant, we were upset. However we figured that if she'd found the right guy, settled down with him and had a baby, that would help her turn her life around. It might give her some stability.'

'And your wife and Lester . . . I see tension here . . . on the fringes at least.'

'Sure,' Garfield said. 'I mean, we'd both been hoping he'd rise to the occasion, but I don't see that happening.'

'Ellie . . . did Ellie confront him? I've seen some flashes that would seem to indicate that.'

Flashes, yeah. Keisha knew that if she had a daughter who'd been knocked up by some no-good layabout, she'd put pressure on him night and day to make sure he did the right thing. This didn't include those times when she would be giving her own daughter hell for getting in this mess. Keisha wouldn't give a guy like that a moment's peace.

It seemed reasonable to assume that Eleanor Garfield might feel the same way.

'Ellie tried to phone the father a few times,' Garfield said. 'But whenever she called his house, she got his mother.' The man frowned. 'Ellie was very upset about the whole situation.'

Keisha thought she might be picking up something else here. 'Ellie *was* upset.' 'Whenever she *called*.' Wendell had started using the past tense when talking about Ellie. Had Garfield already given up on finding his wife? Was he already thinking she was dead?

Keisha told herself she was reading too much into the comments. Garfield was talking about *incidents* that had happened in the past. So speaking of his wife in the past tense made sense, at least in this context.

'Do you think that maybe Lester is involved in my wife's disappearance?' he asked her.

She liked the fact that Wendell was starting to ask her questions. As if she might actually have answers. The hook was firmly set now. He wasn't going to get away. It would be easy to start making him think that way, that maybe his wife had run into Lester and things had turned bad.

However, if Keisha went down that route, it might confirm suspicions that she guessed Garfield already had about her. He might be thinking that she was steering her vision whatever way he led her. She could come back to this later. It was best to go in another direction now and throw him something unexpected.

'The car,' she said.

'What?'

'I keep seeing something about the car.'

'Which car? Lester's car?'

'No, your wife's car. A Nissan.'

'That's right. A 2007. It's silver. What about the car?'

Keisha closed her eyes again. She took her hands off Ellie's robe that was still in her lap and rubbed her forehead. 'It's . . . The car's not on the road.'

Garfield said nothing.

'It's definitely not on the road. It's . . . it's . . .'

Garfield seemed to be holding his breath. 'It's what?' he asked, suddenly impatient. 'If it's not on the road, then where the hell is it?'

Keisha took her fingers away from her head, opened her eyes, and looked the man squarely in the eye.

'I think this is where we have to talk about my fee, Mr Garfield. I believe I'm closing in on something, and it's going to require all my powers of concentration. I don't want to be distracted by wondering whether you're going to do the right thing.'

He ran his tongue around the inside of his mouth and over his teeth.

'You'll take a cheque?'

Seven
Wendell

When Keisha had talked about Ellie being so very cold, he had to admit it had thrown him. However, when she hadn't gone into specifics, he decided it didn't mean anything. It was winter. It was cold. Big deal. It didn't mean the woman was a geniune psychic. She had about as much talent at communicating with the missing and the dead as that weather lady on the six o'clock news did in predicting whether it was going to rain tomorrow.

But then she had mentioned the car. Why had she suddenly wanted to talk about the car? Then she said it was 'definitely not on the road'.

She was right about that.

That car was at the bottom of a lake. No one was going to find it, not for a very, very long time, if ever. The water had to be forty or fifty feet deep there, he bet. It was probably already covered over with ice. It had gotten even colder since Thursday night. It'd be spring before there was a chance of anyone finding it, and even then the odds seemed pretty remote. Someone would have to be diving, right there, to come across it. Even if some fishermen snagged on to it with their lines, it wasn't as if the car was going to float to the surface like an old boot. They'd have to cut their line and put on a new hook.

How could Keisha Ceylon know the car was not on the road?

It could be a lucky guess, as simple as that. But what if it wasn't?

If it wasn't, Garfield saw two possibilities.

One possibility was that this woman actually had the gift of second sight. He'd never bought into this kind of thing before, but who knew? Maybe some people really were born with special powers. Maybe this woman did have visions. How else could you explain that story about Nina, the little girl kidnapped by the neighbour?

So if Keisha had this gift, and she really had a vision about Ellie, then she knew something.

The second possibility – which was no more comforting – was that this psychic thing was an act, a total sham. It was just complete and utter rubbish. She had put on a performance, to cover the fact that, although she had information, it had come to her in a much less mystical way.

She had *seen* what happened, not in a vision, but with her own eyes.

Garfield thought about that as he went into the kitchen to find his cheque book.

She could have been there. She could have been at the lake that night. Maybe she lived in one of the cabins that lined the shore. On his way up there, Garfield had felt confident that being spotted would not be a problem. Most of the places on the lake were seasonal. At this time of year, the cabins were boarded up. By the end of November, almost everyone had turned off the water, poured anti-freeze into the pipes, and put out the mousetraps. Once they had spread around the mothballs, and closed up the shutters, they headed back to their comfortable homes in the city. They would have no plans to return until the spring.

Garfield now had to consider the possibility that one of the cabins had been occupied. Maybe someone had been looking out of their window that night and noticed a car with no lights on, being driven out on to that new ice with only a dusting of snow on it. That sliver of moon gave all the light anyone would need to get an idea of what was going on.

Someone could have seen that car creep out there and stop. Someone could have seen a man get out of the driver's side, with an actual broom in his hand. Someone could have watched as he attempted to sweep away the tyre tracks as made his way back to shore.

Then someone could have seen that same man stop and look back, waiting, *waiting* for the car to plunge through the thin ice.

Garfield shuddered at the memory. The waiting had been like agony. For a few moments there, standing out in the freezing cold, he was convinced the car was not going to go drop through. He had begun to think that it was going to sit there, and that it would still be there in the morning when the sun came out.

It would still be there with his wife's dead body still strapped to the passenger seat.

He'd been talking, earlier in the day, to some customers at the Home Depot store, a couple of fellows who lived up this way. They'd said the lake was starting to freeze over pretty quickly, and that you could already walk out on it, but it wasn't thick enough to take any real weight yet. Some winters, when the ice got thick enough, they'd actually race cars out on the ice. However, they didn't think that would happen until at least February, and only if the temperatures stayed well below freezing.

He didn't think much about it at the time, although the conversation had come back to him later that night.

After it had happened. After she was dead.

When he needed a plan.

Maybe Keisha Ceylon had been there, at the lake. Maybe she had been that someone watching from one of those cabins. When the story about his wife hit the news, she had put it all together.

And now she's here, trying to squeeze money out of me, he thought. It was not quite blackmail. If she were that direct, if she were to say to him, 'I saw what you did, and I'll go to the police with what I know unless you pay me,' she would be taking quite a risk. For all she knew, he wouldn't pay her off to keep her quiet.

He'd just kill her instead.

But using this whole psychic nonsense, that was pure genius. She knew enough to get him curious, to get him worried enough that he'd pay her some money to find out just how much she really knew. Then, once she had the money, she'd keep things just vague enough so that he'd always be left wondering. She'd never have to give away what she knew. She'd never have to admit that she was there. She'd never have to say that, if she wanted to, she could put him in prison for the rest of his life.

Well, Keisha Ceylon wasn't nearly as clever as she thought she was.

Wendell Garfield wasn't interested in taking any chances.

Eight
Melissa

After her father dropped her off and she went up to her apartment, Melissa felt light-headed and sick.

She'd been inside the door only a minute when she suddenly felt very ill. She ran into the bathroom, and dropped to her knees in front of the toilet. She got there just in time.

She cleaned herself up and found herself looking in the mirror. Her hair was dirty and stringy, and there were bags under eyes. She'd hardly slept in the last couple of days. She might have had more sleep than her father, but not much.

Melissa rested her hand on the top of her very pregnant belly, rubbed it, and felt something move around beneath her hand. Then she felt her body begin to shake, her eyes start to moisten. With all the crying she'd done in the last few days, she couldn't believe she had any more tears in her, but they just kept on coming.

She wanted to crawl into bed and never wake up. She'd like to just get under the covers, pull them up over her head, and stay that way for ever. She didn't want to ever have to face the world again.

It was all so terrible.

She couldn't stop thinking about her mother, about her father, about Lester, about the baby, about how her life had spun totally out of control in the last year. It didn't seem to her as if it was going to get any better.

She thought about the press conference. She remembered how strongly her father had felt she should not be a part of it.

'Don't do this,' he'd told her. 'Don't put yourself through it. It's not necessary. I can handle it.'

'No, I should do it.'

'Melissa, I'm telling you—'

'No, Dad, I have to do it. You can't stop me.'

She recalled how he'd gripped her arm and how it had almost hurt. He'd looked into her eyes. 'I'm telling you, it would be a mistake.'

'If I don't do it,' she'd said, 'people will think I don't care.'

And so, reluctantly, he had relented, but he was very firm with her. 'Let me do the talking. I don't want you saying *anything*, you understand? You can cry all you want, but you're not going to say one word.'

So she hadn't. She wasn't sure she could have, anyway. Just as he'd guessed, she cried. The tears were genuine. She hadn't been able to stop. She was so terribly sad. In fact, she was not just sad.

She was scared.

She knew her father loved her very much. She believed that in her heart. But it didn't give her comfort, not now.

He'd told her what to say. He'd rehearsed it with her.

'Your mother went shopping and that's all we know,' he'd said. 'She went off as she always did. Anything could have happened. Maybe she ran off to be with another man, or—'

'Mom would never do that,' Melissa had said, sniffing. She was trying to hold back the tears long enough for her father to drill into her what her story was going to be when the police talked to her. Because the police were going to want to talk to her, she could be sure of that.

'—or maybe that guy who's been doing the car-jackings, maybe he did this. It could have been any number of things. The world is full of disturbed people. The police will have all sorts of theories, and if they never solve it, they never solve it.'

'OK.'

'The main thing is, you just don't know. You have no idea. Are we clear on that?'

'Yes, Daddy.'

She crawled into the bed, lay on her side, and rested her head on the pillow. She grabbed a couple of tissues from the box on her bedside table and dabbed her eyes.

'I can't do this,' she said to herself.

What was it her mother used to tell her?

You have to live your life as if someone's watching you all time. You should behave in a way that means you can never be ashamed.

She turned on to her other side, then back again. It was so hard to get comfortable because of the baby. Finally, she threw back the covers and put her feet on the floor. She sat there on the edge of the bed with her head in her hands.

'I can't do this,' she said again. 'I have to do what's right, no matter who it hurts.'

She wondered, if she should call a lawyer. But she didn't know any lawyers. She didn't want to pick one at random out of the phone book. Was there really any point? If her plan was to tell the truth, did she really need one?

Melissa decided to take a shower first, and

make herself presentable. Before she stepped under the water, she phoned for a taxi. She asked for it to be outside the house in an hour.

She was standing on the curb when the yellow cab came around the corner. When she got in, the driver asked where she'd like to go.

'The police station,' she said.

'OK,' he said, then laughed. 'I was thinking maybe you were going to say the hospital.'

'I've got another couple of months to go,' she said. 'I'm not having a baby in your taxi.'

'That's good to know,' he said and put the car in gear.

She didn't say anything for the rest of the journey. Mostly, she just thought – about how angry her father was going to be with her.

Nine
Keisha

Garfield seemed to take a long time in the kitchen, but when he returned he had a cheque between his thumb and index finger. Keisha smiled as she took it from him, glanced down at it, and saw that it was for the right amount. She folded the cheque once and slipped it into her handbag.

'Is everything all right?' she asked.

'Fine, fine,' he said. 'I couldn't find a pen.'

'You should have asked me. I have a couple in my bag here.'

'I finally found one in the drawer.'

'Well, that's fine.' She put her handbag down on the floor next to the chair. 'Shall I continue?'

'Would you like some coffee?' he asked.

'No, I'm fine, thank you.'

'I was actually just about to make a cup of tea when you knocked on the door. Would you prefer tea?'

'No, thank you.'

Garfield sat down on the settee. 'So, do you live around here?'

Keisha wondered what was going on. She'd brought Garfield right up to the edge of the cliff with that thing about his wife's car not being on the road. She had him then. He was curious, there was no doubt about it.

It was the ideal moment to ask him for the money.

So he'd gone off to the kitchen to write the cheque. And now he was back, ready to continue, and yet he's asking her if she wants coffee? Or tea? Why is he asking her where she lives?

She wondered if he was stalling for time. Had he called the police while he was out of her sight? Had he told them there was this crazy lady in his house, trying to exploit his situation for money?

Keisha didn't think so. She'd have heard something if he'd tried that. He was no more than ten feet away the whole time, just on the other side of the wall. Moreover, the door between the living room and the kitchen was open the entire time.

'I'm sorry, what was the question?' she asked.

'Where do you live?'

'Not far from here,' she said. 'The other side of town.'

He nodded pleasantly. 'Have you lived here long?'

'I moved up here a couple of years ago.'

'Where from?'

'Connecticut. Near New Haven.'

'Do you have a summer place?'

'I've just got the one place, Mr Garfield, and I live in it all year long. Do you want to hear what I have to say, or not? I mean, you've paid me. I'm guessing you'd like to get your money's worth.'

He gave her a go-ahead wave. 'By all means.'

'As I was saying, I've been seeing some kind of flashes of the car your wife was driving.' Keisha still had her hands on the robe, occasionally kneading the fabric between her fingers. 'The silver Nissan.'

'You were saying that the car was not on the road. If it's not on the road, where do you see it?'

Keisha closed her eyes again. 'It's not in a parking lot. I guess that would still count as being on the road, in a way. I'm not seeing it in a garage.'

'What about water?' Garfield asked. 'Do you see any water?'

Curious, Keisha thought. He's just asked if I have a summer place, and now he mentions water. She'd been thinking about Florida earlier. Maybe Garfield was thinking the missus had taken off for Miami. Then again, she'd already suggested that Ellie Garfield was very cold, so if she raised Florida as an option, she was going to get caught out because her story wouldn't make any sense.

She decided to stick with cold. So if it's cold, the water . . . could be frozen.

She opened her eyes for a moment, then closed them again. 'It's funny that you should mention water. I was seeing something, something shimmery, that I thought might be water, but I was thinking maybe it was actually ice.'

'Ice,' Garfield said.

This time, she kept her eyes open. 'Yes, *ice*. Ice in a glass? Ice at a skating rink? Ice, for example, on a lake? Does ice of any kind have any meaning to you? Does it have any significance as far as your wife is concerned?'

'Why should it mean something to me?' he said, a defensive tone edging into his voice.

'You were the one who mentioned water.'

'And then you mentioned ice. I didn't mention ice.'

'But it seems to have some meaning for you,' Keisha said. 'I could see it, in your expression.'

'Why would you say ice on a lake?'

'That was just *one* of the kinds of ice I mentioned. But I can tell there seems to be a connection there.'

Garfield stood up. He took a few steps to the right of the settee, then turned and paced in the other direction. He was stroking the end of his chin, pondering something.

'What is it?' Keisha asked.

He paced back and forth one more time and then stopped. He looked at Keisha, studied her for a moment, then pointed an accusing finger in her direction. 'Maybe it's time you were honest with me.'

'About what?'

'About what's really going on here.'

'I'm sorry, Mr Garfield, but I'm not sure I understand.'

'This whole psychic mumbo-jumbo act of yours is a load of rubbish, isn't it?'

Keisha sighed. 'I told you, if you want to call Nina's father for a reference, I have no problem with that. I'm happy to give you the number.'

'You've got somebody all set up to take the call, haven't you? Is it someone who'll tell me what I want to hear?'

Keisha shook her head and gave him a bruised look. She was trying to appear disappointed and hurt. But what she was thinking was, *At least I've got the money*. The smart thing to do would be to get to the bank when it opens tomorrow morning and cash the cheque, before Garfield had a chance to phone and stop payment on it.

'I'm very sorry you'd think that of me, Mr Garfield. Just when I thought we were making some progress.'

'Whatever you know, whatever you think you know, it's got nothing to do with visions or communicating with the dead or reading tea leaves. Whatever you know, you found it out some other way.'

'I assure you, I—'

'Would you please hand me my wife's robe? I don't want you touching it any more.'

'Oh, certainly,' Keisha said. This really seemed to suggest that they were done.

'Thank you,' he said, gathering it up into a ball.

Keisha reached down for her handbag and set it into her lap. She made sure it was zipped tight at the top, and started to stand.

Garfield said, 'No, don't go yet.'

'I can't see what possible point there would

be in staying any longer, Mr Garfield. It's clear you think I'm some kind of con artist. I've been at this too long to take offence. Some people react like that, and think what I do is a sham. If that's your conclusion, then I'm happy to be on my way.'

She was thinking, *Don't ask me to give you back the money.*

'Did I offend you? I'm very sorry if I did that.' He didn't look at all sincere.

'You just accused me of having someone standing by to – to *lie* to you about my successes. Wouldn't you expect me to take offence at that?'

He was still pacing, still fondling the robe, doing something with it, as if it was a mound of clay that he was shaping into something. Keisha watched as he took a few steps one way, then the other. It struck her that this was how he formed his thoughts, by making these little journeys around the room.

'You *are* very clever, I have to give you that,' he said.

Keisha said nothing. She was starting to get an inkling of what was going on. She should have caught on a little sooner.

'Very, very clever,' he said, stepping over to the window, and pulling back the curtain to get a look at the street. This meant he was standing off to one side and slightly behind Keisha, and she had to twist around in her chair to see him. 'I'd like to apologise. Forget what I just said. Why don't you carry on, let me hear some more about your *vision.*'

'Mr Garfield, I'm not sure—'

'No, no, please, go on.'

Keisha put her bag back down on the carpet and rested her hands by her thighs on the seat cushion. 'Would you like me to start again with the ice, or move on to something else?'

'Why don't you just say whatever comes into your head.'

Keisha had a bad feeling. She couldn't recall dealing with anyone like this before, who'd seemingly lost interest in what she had to say, wanted her to leave, then had a change of heart. Judging by his tone now, she didn't believe he was even interested in anything else she had to say.

He just didn't want her to leave.

Something was very wrong here. Suddenly she thought she knew why.

It's him. He did it.

It explained his strange behaviour. Keisha wanted to kick herself for not realising it sooner. She'd been at this long enough, of course, to know that when a wife was murdered – or missing – the husband was always a prime suspect. It wasn't very often that people were killed by strangers. They were killed by people they knew. Wives were killed by husbands. Husbands were killed by wives.

The man had moved away from the window, and was taking a route behind Keisha's chair. She was going to have to turn around to keep her eye on him.

'On second thought, sure, tell me about the ice.'

The televised news conference had put her on the wrong track. She'd figured, first of all, that if the police had suspected strongly that Garfield had killed his wife, they'd have never let him go before the cameras. Would they? She had to admit, he was good. Those tears looked real. The way he took his pregnant daughter into his arms to comfort her, that was pretty convincing, too.

It had never occurred to Keisha before that the people she preyed upon could be anything other than innocent. Guilty people often made the best targets. They could be so eager to prove that they were as much in the dark as everyone else that they leaped at the chance to pay to hear what she had to say.

They would tell themselves, *I look so innocent. A real murderer would never do this, right?*

Maybe that explained why, at first, Garfield had agreed to listen to her. But something had happened during their conversation. Things had shifted. He'd become anxious. Had she actually hit on something by accident?

Was it when she said his wife was cold? Or was it when she said something about the car being off the road? Had those comments been close enough to the truth to make Garfield think that she was on to something?

It was time for Keisha to leave. Maybe – and she couldn't believe she was even thinking of this – she should even give him back his money. Perhaps she should say something like, 'You know what? Whatever vision I may have had, it's gone. I'm not picking up anything. The signals have faded. The flashes, they're over. So I think the best thing to do would be for me to return your money and I'll just be on my—'

But just then, there was a flash of pink before her eyes. It was not a vision this time, though. It was the sash, from the robe.

And now Garfield was looping it around her neck and drawing it tight.

Ten

Melissa

Before Melissa would tell her story to the detective, whose name was Marshall – which struck her as funny, a policeman named Marshall – she wanted assurances that the police would go easy on her father.

'There are reasons that might explain why he did what he did?'

Marshall, seated across the table from her in the interview room, said, 'It's hard for us to make promises where your dad is concerned when we don't know exactly what it is that he's done.'

'I don't want to get him in trouble,' Melissa said. 'Even though I know that's probably what's going to happen.'

'But he knows something about what really happened to your mother,' he said. 'That *is* why you're here.'

'In a way,' Melissa said. 'You know what? I

know I only just sat down, but I really have to pee.'

'Sure, OK,' Marshall said. 'Let me show you where to go.'

Melissa went to the bathroom and a couple of minutes later the two of them were back sitting across from each other. Melissa had one hand on the table and the other on her belly.

'I really love my dad,' she said. 'I really do.'

'Of course. And I bet you love your mom, too.'

Melissa looked down.

'Melissa,' Detective Marshall said gently. 'Can you tell me . . . is your mother still alive?' She mumbled something so softly that he couldn't hear what she'd said. 'What was that?'

'No.'

'No, she's not alive?'

'That's right. But if I tell you everything, you have to promise to be nice to Dad. Because he's a good man, really.'

'As I said, Melissa, without knowing the facts—'

'I don't want to get him into trouble. He's already going to be really mad at me.'

'We can make sure he doesn't hurt you.'

'He wouldn't hurt me, but he's going to be pissed off.'

'I can certainly understand that,' the detective said. 'But I'm guessing you're thinking that, sometimes, you have to do what's right.'

'Yeah, I've kind of been thinking that too.'

'And you want to do right by your mother.'

'Yeah, I've been thinking that, too.'

'Why don't we start with you telling me where your mother is.'

'She's in the car.'

The detective nodded. 'This would be your mother's car. The Nissan.'

'That's right.'

'And where's the car, Melissa?'

'It's at the bottom of the lake.'

The detective nodded again. 'OK. What lake would that be?'

'I don't know the name of it, but I think I could show you how to get there. It's about an hour's drive, I think. Although, even if I take you there, I don't know where *exactly* it is in the lake. And the ice has probably already frozen over. It's been cold. I just know she's in the lake. In the car.'

'OK, that's OK, we have divers for that kind of thing.'

Melissa looked surprised. 'They can go in the water even when it's super cold?'

'Oh yeah, they've got these special wetsuits that help keep them warm.'

'I couldn't do that. I couldn't swim in freezing-cold water. I can't even go in a pool unless it's heated to eighty-five or ninety degrees.'

Marshall gave her a warm smile. 'That's like my wife. It's got to be almost as hot as a sauna before she'll get in. So, Melissa, your father, he put the car in the water?'

'Yep. He drove the car out on to the lake, where the ice was thin. Then he waited for the car to go through.' She started to weep. 'And then it did.'

'How do you know this, Melissa? Did your father tell you what he did?'

'I saw it. I saw the car go through the ice.'

'Where were you?'

'I was on the shore, watching.' A solitary tear ran down her cheek. She bit her lip, trying to hold herself together. 'I feel really bad, but I also feel a bit better, you know? Coming here and telling you what happened has helped.'

'Of course it has.'

'It's not the kind of secret I could keep.'

'Melissa, you must realise we're going to have to go out to his house and talk to your father. First, I need to ask you, does he keep any guns in the house?'

'No, I don't think so. He's never been interested in guns.'

'We just don't want to have to hurt him, you know? When we go out there, we want to be able to bring him in peacefully. Do you think he's dangerous?'

She was puzzled by the question and shook her head. 'He's not dangerous. I mean, it's not like he's ever killed anybody or anything.'

'You mean, before your mother.'

'Oh, he didn't kill my mother. Is that what you were thinking? I guess I should start at the beginning.'

Eleven
Keisha

When Keisha Ceylon saw the pink sash drop past her eyes, she reached up instinctively to get her fingers between it and her neck. But she wasn't quick enough. Wendell Garfield wrapped it tightly around her throat and began to twist.

'I swear, I don't know how you know, but you're not going to tell anyone,' he said.

Keisha clawed at the sash, her fingernails ripping into her own skin as she tried to loosen his hold on her. The satiny ribbon was already cutting deep into her neck and there wasn't a hope of getting her fingers underneath it.

Garfield was leaning down over her, his mouth close to her right ear. His breath was hot against her cheek.

She tried to say something, to scream, but with her windpipe being squeezed, nothing came out, not a sound. She felt her eyes bulging.

She kicked at the floor, digging into the carpet with her heels.

Keisha Ceylon knew that she was going to die. She didn't need any vision for that glimpse into the future.

Any second now, she thought, it's going to be over. *Maybe I had it coming. I've been ripping people off, taking advantage of them when they were at their most vulnerable. I'm getting what I deserve.*

It didn't make her feel any better about it, though.

She gave up clawing at her throat and dropped her hands to her side.

'You must have been there,' Garfield said through gritted teeth. 'You had to be watching. That's the only way I can understand it. You were up there, you saw me put the car on the ice, you saw it go under, and then you thought you could blackmail me. You'd ask for a thousand today, another thousand next week, and then another the week after that, until I had nothing left.'

He had the ends of the sash twisted several times around his palms and kept pulling. Keisha could feel herself starting to faint, to black out. She wondered what he would do with her body. He hoped he wouldn't put her in the lake along with Mrs Garfield.

She didn't like water.

In the seconds just before it seemed to her that she was going to lose consciousness, her fingers dug into the seat of her chair.

Her right hand brushed up against something.

Something soft, almost furry.

Knitting yarn.

And as her fingers fumbled across the ball of wool, they landed on something else. It was long, and narrow, and pointed, like a stick, or a needle.

A knitting needle.

In the last second Keisha had before she blacked out, she grabbed hold of the knitting needle with her right hand and swung her hand up and over her shoulder. She swung it as hard as she could.

The scream was only an inch from her ear. It was horrific.

As the grip on Keisha's neck slackened, she tumbled forward out of the chair. She collapsed on to the floor, gasping for breath. She was on her knees, one hand on the floor supporting her, the other on her neck. Air rushed into her lungs so quickly that it hurt. Her gasps would have been loud enough to hear from anywhere in the house, were it not for Wendell Garfield's cries of agony.

Keisha, even as she struggled to get her breath back, had to turn and see what she had done.

The knitting needle was sticking straight out of Garfield's right eye. Blood poured from the socket, covering the right side of his face. Judging by how much of the needle remained exposed, Keisha thought that a good four to five inches of it was buried in his head.

However, he could see her with his left eye and, still screaming, he started coming around the chair after her.

Keisha struggled to her feet and started moving towards the door. She hit her knee going around the corner of the coffee table and stumbled, allowing Garfield to get close enough to clamp his hand on to her arm.

'You bitch!' Garfield said, although there was so much blood in his throat it sounded as though he was gargling.

Garfield yanked so hard on her arm that Keisha went down on to the floor again. She ended up sprawled on her back. Before she had a chance to roll away, he landed on top of her, straddling her middle.

He didn't have the sash any more. He was going to have to make do with his hands.

He leaned forward, the knitting needle still sticking out of his eye socket, blood dripping on to Keisha, and got his fingers and thumbs around her neck. She flailed about, but his hands had her neck pinned to the floor.

She started passing out all over again. With her last ounce of strength, she took the heel of her hand and shot it straight up against the end of the knitting needle.

She drove it into Garfield's head another three inches.

There was another scream, and then, for a moment, he seemed to freeze above her. His grip on her neck relaxed, his arms went weak, and his body collapsed on top of her.

Keisha didn't even take a second to get her breath back this time. She pushed frantically at his dead body until she had flung it off her and crawled a few feet away. Only then, once she was able to breathe normally again, did she decide she was entitled to take a moment and break down in hysterics.

Twelve
Melissa

'You're sure you don't want a lawyer?' Detective Marshall asked.

'I'm positive,' Melissa Garfield said. 'I'm going to plead guilty to everything.'

'Then you have to sign here. And here.'

Melissa scribbled her signature.

'OK, then why don't you start from the beginning.'

'You see,' Melissa said, 'instead of going shopping first, Mom decided to visit me. She'd do that once in a while, just drop by without calling or anything beforehand. She'd say, "What, can't a mother pop in and visit her daughter?" She comes in when I'm in the kitchen. I'm cutting up some celery and carrot sticks to put in a salad because I'm actually trying to eat the right things so the baby will be healthy, you know, even though I'd rather just be eating pizza and burgers, but I'm *trying*, OK? I'm really trying.'

'Sure,' the detective said.

'It's like she was checking up on me all the time. She was always asking me these questions, like what's happening with Lester and was he going to marry me and help me take care of the baby. She'd say, maybe I could move in with him and his mom and dad, then she'd be able to help me look after the baby, like I was really going to do that, right? And then she wanted to know if I'd applied to the vet school I was talking about, because I happened to mention it, you know. I said, not yet, but I was thinking about it. She said, what's the hold-up? She wanted to know why I couldn't just go on the computer and press a couple of buttons. Then I'd be enrolled. If it was that easy, she said, I should just go and do it now.

'I said, Please Mom, will you just give me some room to breathe, you know? I've got a baby coming in a few weeks and I've got a lot on my mind. OK, maybe I'm thinking about it, but do I have to do something about it right this very second? And she said, it'll take you just two minutes, so why don't you do it? I'll cut up your celery and your carrots for you. Then she tried to take the knife from me. I don't know what happened but I kind of snapped or something, you know?'

'I hear you,' the detective said.

'So, I don't know how exactly it happened, but the knife went into her. Then I guess I must have put it into her a second time and then she looks at me and she's all, like, what have you done? Then she falls down and she doesn't move or anything.'

'So what did you do then? Did you think about calling for an ambulance?'

'I guess I went crazy for a while, you know? But I managed to call my dad.'

'OK.'

'I said, something's happened to Mom. You have to get over here. He said, is it a heart attack or something? I said, no. He said I should call the ambulance. Then I said that I'd stabbed her, and he shouted "What?" Then he told me I shouldn't do anything and he'd come right over.'

'To help you out.'

Melissa nodded. 'So he came over really quickly, and he was kind of all freaked out. He took one look at Mom and he could see that she was dead. He said he had to think. I asked him, was I going to go to jail? Was I going to have my baby in jail? He kept telling me to shut up, because he was thinking, and then he had this idea. He took Mom out of the apartment the back way and got her into her car. Then he told me I was going to have to follow in his car and drive along after him. I followed him up to this lake. He put the car on the ice and it went through. I guess I already told you about that part.'

'And then what happened?'

'Dad came back to my place and cleaned up. There was blood all over the place. It was horrible. It took hours to clean up the blood. I couldn't do it. I stayed in my bed, under the covers. When he was finished he told me everything was going to be OK. He said I wasn't going to have to go to jail.'

She smiled sadly. 'He said he loved me very much and he wanted everything to be OK for me. He said I'd done a bad thing but sometimes people made mistakes and he didn't want my whole life to be ruined, you know? He's a really good dad. He said the police would just think Mom ran away, or maybe she got killed by that car-jacker guy. He said they'd never really know what happened because they'd never be able to find Mom's car. And if the police didn't know what happened, they couldn't really charge anyone.'

Melissa shook her head.

'He's going to be so angry with me, because

he did all this to protect me, and now . . . Well, here I am. But I just . . . I can't do it. I feel bad about what I did. I really loved my mom.'

Detective Marshall reached out and touched her hand. 'I know.'

'Is my dad going to be in a lot of trouble?'

'Well, I'd have to say yes, but with the right lawyer, and a sympathetic jury . . . A lot of them will understand the lengths a father might go to, to help his daughter. He might have to go to jail, but maybe not for a long time.'

'Not as long as me.'

Detective Marshall nodded. 'You might be right about that.'

For the first time since she'd been in this room, a shadow of a smile crossed Melissa's lips.

'That'd be OK. As long as he doesn't have to spend the rest of his life in jail. That wouldn't be fair. He's not that old. He's got a lot of time left in him.'

Thirteen
Keisha

She wasn't going to call the police.

She knew it was self-defense. She knew it wasn't murder. However, she didn't have any confidence that the police would see it that way. They certainly wouldn't, once they started looking into her background and saw her convictions for fraud back in 1999 and 2003 in Connecticut. It would be the end of her if they started figuring out what kind of trick she'd been hoping to play on Wendell Garfield. Even if the guy did murder his wife, they'd find something to charge her with.

Keisha hadn't told anyone she was coming here. She'd put her boyfriend on alert, and told him he might have to be the reference for the Nina story. Yet she had never told him where she was going, or whom she was going to see. The Garfield house was on a street where the houses were pretty spread out. She thought there was a good chance no one had seen her get out of her car and come into the house. If she could get out of here and back into her car unseen, she'd be all right.

Fingerprints.

She wondered what she'd touched. The robe, but it wouldn't hold a fingerprint. Surely the police couldn't lift a print off the fabric of the chair.

Just to be sure, she wiped down the coffee table and any other surfaces she thought she might have touched. There was plenty of blood around, but none of it was hers, so she thought she'd be OK as far as DNA tests were concerned.

Once she got home, she'd get out of these blood-soaked clothes and burn them.

Keisha had a good feeling about this. She believed she could walk away and no one would ever know she was here.

Wendell Garfield, sprawled out across the floor, certainly wouldn't be talking.

She'd have to wear a scarf at her neck for a few weeks. She'd caught a look at herself in the mirror. There was a purple ring around her throat.

'No more of this vision nonsense,' she said to herself. 'No more.'

This was a message, no doubt about it. Keisha had never been a particularly religious person, but this certainly felt like a warning from the man upstairs. 'Stop it,' he was telling her.

She was going to stop.

'Lord, just let me walk out of here and I'm yours,' she said.

She took one last look at the room, at Garfield's dead body, just to be sure she hadn't missed anything. She was OK. She was as sure as she could be.

Keisha slipped out of the house, wiping down the door handle on her way. She was halfway across the yard when she happened to reach up and touch her ear.

There was nothing dangling from it.

She reached up and touched her other ear. The parrot earring was there but the other one was gone.

It had been lost in the house.

'Oh God,' she said under her breath. She had to go back inside.

She went back to the door and stood there a moment, steeling herself. She went in, and took in the scene all over again. She started by the chair where she had been sitting. She patted around it, sticking her fingers down into the cracks between the cushions.

No luck.

She looked at the coffee table, and scanned

the carpets. The earring was nowhere to be seen.

There was only one place left to look.

Keisha got down on her knees next to the body, slipped her hands under him, and rolled him over. The carpet was completely soaked with the blood that had poured out of Garfield's eye.

She spotted a small bump in the pool of blood. She stuck her fingers into it and lifted up her earring. The parrot looked a seagull caught in a red oil spill. She dropped the earring into her handbag, and went back out the front door.

She got in her car.

She got her keys out of her bag.

She turned the key in the ignition.

As she was driving away, looking ahead, she saw a police car turn the corner.

No no no no.

As it approached, Keisha wondered how visible the bloodstains were, splattered across the front of her dress. Would the policeman notice them as they passed each other? Why hadn't she had her car windows tinted?

The police car got closer. There were two officers inside. A woman was behind the wheel, with a man in the passenger seat.

Just look ahead, she told herself, as if you don't care. Be cool.

The cars came alongside one another.

As the police car slid past, Keisha was certain no one looked across at her. She kept her eyes to the front. Then, seconds later, she glanced in the rear-view mirror, expecting the patrol car's brake lights to come on. At any moment, the car would turn around and come after her, its lights flashing.

Nothing happened. The police car drove on, pulling over to the side of the road out in front of the Garfield house.

Keisha put on her indicator, and turned left at the corner.

She was safe.

It was a lesson learned.

Fourteen
Winona

She'd drifted off during a TV wildlife special. It was something about the rain forests. She'd never been all that interested in the rain forests.

Only a few minutes into sleep, Winona Simpson woke with a start.

Her heart was pounding. She reached under the various necklaces she always wore and put her palm between her breasts, to feel the rapid beating.

That was some nightmare.

It was so real, so frightening.

No, she thought, it was not a nightmare.

It was something else.

She'd had a vision. That was the way they often came to her – as she slept.

Winona blinked a couple of times, trying to bring into focus the images in her head.

She drew in a sharp breath.

'Oh, Keisha,' she said. 'What on earth have you done?'

Quick Reads

Books in the Quick Reads series

101 Ways to get your Child to Read	Patience Thomson
All These Lonely People	Gervase Phinn
Black-Eyed Devils	Catrin Collier
Bloody Valentine	James Patterson
Buster Fleabags	Rolf Harris
The Cave	Kate Mosse
Chickenfeed	Minette Walters
Cleanskin	Val McDermid
Clouded Vision	Linwood Barclay
A Cool Head	Ian Rankin
Danny Wallace and the Centre of the Universe	Danny Wallace
The Dare	John Boyne
Doctor Who: Code of the Krillitanes	Justin Richards
Doctor Who: I Am a Dalek	Gareth Roberts
Doctor Who: Made of Steel	Terrance Dicks
Doctor Who: Revenge of the Judoon	Terrance Dicks
Doctor Who: The Sontaran Games	Jacqueline Rayner
Dragons' Den: Your Road to Success	
A Dream Come True	Maureen Lee
Follow Me	Sheila O'Flanagan
Girl on the Platform	Josephine Cox
The Grey Man	Andy McNab
The Hardest Test	Scott Quinnell
Hell Island	Matthew Reilly

Hello Mum	Bernardine Evaristo
How to Change Your Life in 7 Steps	John Bird
Humble Pie	Gordon Ramsay
Jack and Jill	Lucy Cavendish
Kung Fu Trip	Benjamin Zephaniah
Last Night Another Soldier	Andy McNab
Life's New Hurdles	Colin Jackson
Life's Too Short	Val McDermid, Editor
Lily	Adèle Geras
Men at Work	Mike Gayle
Money Magic	Alvin Hall
My Dad's a Policeman	Cathy Glass
One Good Turn	Chris Ryan
The Perfect Holiday	Cathy Kelly
The Perfect Murder	Peter James
RaW Voices: True Stories of Hardship	Vanessa Feltz
Reaching for the Stars	Lola Jaye
Reading My Arse!	Ricky Tomlinson
Star Sullivan	Maeve Binchy
Strangers on the 14:02	Priya Basil
The Sun Book of Short Stories	
Survive the Worst and Aim for the Best	Kerry Katona
The 10 Keys to Success	John Bird
Tackling Life	Charlie Oatway
The Tannery	Sherrie Hewson
Traitors of the Tower	Alison Weir
Trouble on the Heath	Terry Jones
Twenty Tales from the War Zone	John Simpson
We Won the Lottery	Danny Buckland

Quick Reads

Great stories, great writers, great entertainment

Quick Reads are brilliantly written short new books by bestselling authors and celebrities. Whether you're an avid reader who wants a quick fix or haven't picked up a book since school, sit back, relax and let Quick Reads inspire you.

We would like to thank all our partners in the Quick Reads project for their help and support:

Arts Council England
The Department for Business, Innovation and Skills
NIACE
unionlearn
National Book Tokens
The Reading Agency
National Literacy Trust
Welsh Books Council
Basic Skills Cymru, Welsh Assembly Government
The Big Plus Scotland
DELNI
NALA

Quick Reads would also like to thank the Department for Business, Innovation and Skills; Arts Council England and World Book Day for their sponsorship and NIACE for their outreach work.

Quick Reads is a World Book Day initiative.

www.quickreads.org.uk www.worldbookday.com

Quick Reads

Great stories, great writers, great entertainment

Follow Me

Sheila O'Flanagan

Headline Review

The romantic tale of a career girl, a handsome stranger and chips

Pippa Jones is 20-something and single. She likes chips, country music and her cat. She also loves her career as number one sales rep for a computer firm. The only thing she hasn't got time for is men. Broken-hearted last time round, Pippa is sticking to girlfriends – and winning a dream trip to New York.

However, life isn't that simple. A rival firm is stealing her clients, and a tall, fair stranger is following her everywhere. He's in the bar, at dinner, even at her meetings. Is he a stalker? Whoever he is, he's about to turn Pippa's world upside down.

Quick Reads

Great stories, great writers, great entertainment

Kung Fu Trip

Benjamin Zephaniah

Bloomsbury

A crazy martial arts adventure

From the moment Benjamin Zephaniah meets the 'kissy kissy' woman in his Chinese hotel, you know this isn't going to be an ordinary tourist story. Benjamin visits master Iron Breath to learn the secrets of Kung Fu – but it's not going to be easy, or cheap. Is he going to be ripped off? Would it be better to see Fat Thumb and his Smelly Finger? Why does everyone want him to sing like Eddy Grant? One thing's for sure, it's all a lot different to home.

Kung Fu Trip is a little bit daft and a whole lot of fun.

Quick Reads

Great stories, great writers, great entertainment

Bloody Valentine

James Patterson

Arrow

This year Valentine's Day isn't for romance.
It's for murder

Mega-rich restaurant owner Jack Barnes and his second wife Zee are very much in love. However, their plans for Valentine's Day are about to be torn apart by the most violent murder. Who is the strange figure plotting this sick crime? Who hates Jack that much? There are plenty of suspects living in Jack's fancy block of flats. Is it them, or could it be the work of an outsider with a twisted mind? One thing's for sure, the police have got their work cut out solving this bloody mess.

This gory murder mystery will make you feel weak at the knees.

Quick Reads

Great stories, great writers, great entertainment

Jack and Jill

Lucy Cavendish

Penguin

The disturbing tale of a young boy
and his devoted sister

Jill loves her little brother, Jack. She understands what he's thinking, which is just as well because Jack won't speak.

There are plenty of things Jill doesn't understand though. Why is her mum dumping her and Jack in the country? Why did her dad leave and she's not allowed to talk about it? She doesn't know why her aunt and uncle give her and Jack strange looks, or why they're being talked about in the village.

With a local country boy Jill decides to find out what's going on and uncovers the appalling truth behind brother Jack's silence.

Quick Reads

Great stories, great writers, great entertainment

Men at Work

Mike Gayle

Hodder

A sweet, funny story about love and work

Ian Greening loves his job. He loves it so much he won't even take a promotion. He'd rather muck about with his workmates.

The other love of his life is girlfriend Emma. They've been together for years. The problems start when Emma loses her job and gets a new one in Ian's office. Ian doesn't like it at all. No more mucking about. No more flirting with the girls in admin. Ian wants her out. The question is, how? Can he do it without losing her or will it all end in tears?

Other resources

Enjoy this book? Find out about all the others from **www.quickreads.org.uk**

Free courses are available for anyone who wants to develop their skills. You can attend the courses in your local area. If you'd like to find out more, phone 0800 66 0800.

Don't get by get on 0800 66 0800

For more information on developing your basic skills in Scotland, call The Big Plus free on 0808 100 1080 or visit www.thebigplus.com

Join the Reading Agency's Six Book Challenge at www.sixbookchallenge.org.uk

Publishers Barrington Stoke (www.barringtonstoke.co.uk) and New Island (www.newisland.ie) also provide books for new readers.

The BBC runs an adult basic skills campaign. See www.bbc.co.uk/raw.

www.worldbookday.com